Published by Creative Education
123 South Broad Street, Mankato, Minnesota 56001
Creative Education is an imprint of The Creative Company

Designed by Stephanie Blumenthal
Production Design by The Design Lab
Editorial Assistance by Lori LaChapelle

Photos by: AP/Wide World Photos, DMI Photography,
Everett Collection, FPG International, Globe Photos, Retna Ltd.,
Shooting Star, Tuskegee University

Library of Congress Cataloging-in-Publication Data

Chapman, Kathleen Ferguson.
Spike Lee / by Kathleen Ferguson Chapman
p. cm. — (Ovations)
Summary: Describes the life of the black filmmaker from
his childhood to his current career.
ISBN 0-88682-697-7

1. Lee, Spike—Juvenile literature. 2. Afro-American motion picture
producers and directors—Biography—Juvenile literature. [1. Lee, Spike
2. Motion picture producers and directors. 3. Afro-Americans—Biography.]
I. Title. II. Series: Ovations (Mankato, Minn.)

PN1998.3.L44C46   1999
791.43'0233'092   93-48821
[b]—dc21

First edition

2   4   6   8   9   7   5   3   1

SPIKE

LEE

BY KATHLEEN FERGUSON CHAPMAN

Creative Education

REFLECTIONS

When Spike Lee strides
down his hometown streets
of Brooklyn, he doesn't look like a
flashy movie star and internationally
known director. Passersby who spot
him hurrying along are likely to see
a man dressed in stone-washed jeans,
a sweatshirt or T-shirt, Nike shoes,
an ear stud, and a baseball cap.

This slightly-built yet steely
and determined man offers clues to
his identity, however, when he wears
a jacket or cap promoting his latest
film, as he often likes to do. And his
well-recognized face, distinguished by
glasses, a short beard, and mustache,
has become something of a pop culture icon in recent years.

His appearance might not match what people think a successful filmmaker and actor should look like, but Spike Lee is a nonconformist. His appearance and his work don't always fit in with what people think is usual. And that's fine with him.

Some observers have said Lee is among the most innovative directors of his generation, while others have sharply criticized his work. Some African-Americans have complained that he has revealed too much about their private failures and foibles, while others feel he has shown the richness of African-American thought and culture. Indignant movie viewers have called him many names, ranging from "arrogant" to "racist" and "sexist." Admirers have praised him for opening people's eyes to the prejudices and stereotypes long perpetuated in our culture.

So just who is Spike Lee? Is he a far-seeing social critic, an avant-garde artist, a pop star whose time in the limelight will pass? As Lee himself once said to a reporter, "Look, I make films. I don't have time to give sound bites to journalists who want to know what I'm about. . . . I'm a filmmaker first and foremost. That's what I do; that's what makes me happy."

Despite his unassuming physical presence, Spike Lee stands tall as both an innovative leader in the film industry and a determined spokesman for the African-American community.

EVOLUTION

In the early 1800s two American slaves, living on separate South Carolina plantations, fell deeply in love and were married. Mike and Phoebe had seven children together and were expecting their eighth when Phoebe's owner moved to Alabama, taking her away from her devastated husband. Mike worked determinedly for years to accomplish a nearly impossible feat for a slave: saving the staggering sum of $1,900 that would buy his freedom. When he was finally able to buy his freedom, he headed to Alabama to find his love. Joyously reunited, Phoebe and Mike had another 40 years of marriage and three more children together.

One of their great-grand children, William James Edwards, also overcame great odds. Though faced with a crippling bone disease

and living in poverty, he worked and raised the money he needed to attend Booker T. Washington's Tuskegee Institute in Alabama, starting in 1889. That education led to success and he later founded the Snow Hill Institute, an outstanding and influential school for black youths.

Ⓞne of his grandchildren, Bill Lee, achieved his own success in the early 1960s as an acclaimed jazz bassist, performing with stars ranging from Billie Holliday to Bob Dylan. When electrified music became popular, however, he refused to play the electric bass, which limited his work opportunities and put serious financial strains on his family. But his wife, Jacquelyn Shelton Lee, worked steadfastly as a teacher of art and black literature, earning money to support the family and allowing Bill to stand by his principles as a jazz purist. Together they passed on their determination and drive to their firstborn son, Shelton Jackson Lee, who as an infant quickly earned the nickname "Spike" from his mother for being such a "tough baby."

"You can see where [Spike Lee] gets his drive," wrote Rick Reilly, a reporter for *Sports Illustrated*. "And all that anger, too. And brilliance and doggedness and burden." Reilly reported the story about Lee's slave forebears and traced the famous director's roots after Lee loaned him a treasured book

Spike Lee lives his life proudly in the tradition of his great-grandfather, William James Edwards, who rose from an ancestry of slavery to gain education. Spike's own success has been supported by his family, including sister Joie Lee, left.

about his ancestors, *Fallen Prince* by Donald P. Stone. Reilly points out that this family history says a lot about Spike Lee. "A legacy of will began with Mike and Phoebe, ran through Willie Edwards . . . and Bill Lee, and now courses through Spike Lee. He springs from American black royalty."

CAREER DECISIONS

Born in Atlanta on March 20, 1957, Spike Lee was the first of four sons and one daughter that Bill and Jacquelyn Lee would have together. Bill moved his growing family to the jazz mecca of Chicago and then in 1959 joined other jazz musicians in New York. The Lees settled in Brooklyn, first living in Crown Heights and then moving to Cobble Hill, where they were the first blacks in the neighborhood. "I was called 'nigger' the first day we moved in," Spike recalled, "but after that, when they saw we were no threat, I had all Italian friends."

The Lees eventually bought a brownstone in Fort Greene, a Brooklyn neighborhood where Spike, despite his financial success, still chooses to live today. (His production and record companies, 40 Acres and a Mule Filmworks and Musicworks, are also located there.) Though the family struggled some over the years, the Lees were better off than many other Fort Greene residents. Nonetheless, Spike Lee certainly grew up aware of the devastating economic and social problems faced by many African-Americans. And thanks to his family, he also learned to appreciate the richness and vitality of black culture.

Bill introduced his children to African-American music, sometimes taking them to his performances at jazz clubs and music festivals. Jacquelyn insisted that her children read black literature, and she took them to plays, movies, and all-black art exhibits. Her creativity was also evident in her writing.

"I have a stack of letters she wrote to me when I was in college," Spike said. "She had a great sense of humor, and her letters were funny."

Though Spike enjoyed going to the movies, he dreamed of becoming an athlete, not a filmmaker. "I had no idea that people made movies," he wrote in the book *Five for Five: The Films of Spike Lee.* "Movies were magic—and something you couldn't do. Or so you thought."

Lee didn't decide that he'd like to make movies himself until his college years, when he followed family tradition and attended Morehouse College, a prestigious black institution in Atlanta. He majored in mass communications and watched films in his spare time. During his sophomore year he began playing around with a movie camera and started to experiment with the art of filmmaking.

After graduating from Morehouse in 1979, Lee entered New York University's renowned Institute of Film and Television at the Tisch School of the Arts. For his first-year project, Lee made a ten-minute film titled *The Answer,* about a black screenwriter hired to direct a remake of D. W. Griffith's classic film, *Birth of a Nation.* The film criticized Griffith, whose

Despite Spike's success in the film and music industries, his loyalty to his roots has never wavered. He still lives and works in a modest building, above, in the Brooklyn neighborhood in which he grew up.

work many people respected. Lee believed that his treatment of "the father of cinema" offended his instructors, who were not happy with the film. Members of the faculty came close to asking Lee to leave film school. But, they insist, they wanted him to leave only because they felt he didn't demonstrate good filmmaking skills on the project.

Lee went on to prove his abilities with his master's thesis film, a forty-five-minute piece entitled *Joe's Bed-Stuy Barbershop: We Cut Heads.* The film was about a barber in Brooklyn's impoverished Bedford-Stuyvesant neighborhood who becomes involved in illegal gambling. The film won a student Academy Award and was the first student project to be included in Lincoln Center's "New Directors/New Films" series.

FILMS WITH A PURPOSE

After graduating from film school in 1982, Lee took a job cleaning and shipping film at a movie distribution house, earning $200 a week. In his spare time he worked in his basement apartment on ideas for movie scripts. Then, in the summer of 1984, he attempted to make a movie based on a script he wrote about a black bicycle messenger in Brooklyn. Lee hired actors and a crew and was prepared to start shooting *Messenger* when some significant funding fell through and his plans collapsed. He was forced to

Spike Lee's work behind the camera as a controversial film director has made him a high profile celebrity, but his casual clothes, baseball caps, and down-to-earth personality make him an approachable star.

cancel the project after spending more than $40,000 (including $20,000 from his grandmother Zimmie) and eight weeks on preproduction.

The failure devastated Lee, but it made him more determined than ever to produce a film. He decided to scale down his plans and shoot an inexpensive movie with just a few characters and very little location work. He got his chance the following summer with a comedy called *She's Gotta Have It*. The story focused on a young African-American woman, Nola Darling, who has relationships with three men at the same time (including fast-talking Mars Blackmon, played by Lee). The young director said he wanted to "make an intelligent film that showed black people loving each other and black people falling out of love."

Lee and his cast and crew (which included family members, as in several later films) shot the movie in twelve days. Lee and a close friend from college, Monty Ross, begged and borrowed money from everyone they could think of. They spent just $175,000 to make the picture, which turned out to be a major hit, winning the Prix de la Jeunesse (award for newcomers) at the Cannes Film Festival. *She's Gotta Have It* grossed more than $7 million and became the first movie by an independent African-American filmmaker to win major international distribution since the early 1970s.

Spike Lee's film credits include She's Gotta Have It, *left, and the critically acclaimed* Do the Right Thing, *opposite, in which Spike also starred.*

Lee's second major film, a musical comedy called *School Daze*, got mixed reviews but was highly profitable. This film took a comedic look at black college life and challenged views on self-identity and self-esteem— exploring interracial prejudice among blacks.

But his third movie, the powerful *Do the Right Thing*, grabbed the nation's attention. This highly praised comedy-drama focused on conflicts that arise between ethnic groups, especially African-Americans and Italian-Americans, uneasily living together in Brooklyn's Bedford-Stuyvesant neighborhood. The 1986 New York murder of a black man by a group of whites partly inspired Lee. His movie's plot culminates when a group of white police officers kill a black man. Outraged blacks then destroy a neighborhood Italian-American pizzeria.

Some critics warned that the film would provoke race riots. People argued about whether the character Mookie (played by Lee), who leads the charge on the pizzeria, "did the right thing." Lee said that the film revealed the racism of some movie critics. He wrote that "some of these critics were more concerned about Sal's Pizzeria burning down than they were with a human life—a black human life."

Do the Right Thing further assured Lee's status as a controversial celebrity. Lee has responded to his fame with mixed emotions. He has taken advantage of his high visibility to air his outspoken views. But he has frequently reacted with exasperation to reporters' questions about where he chooses to live. "Who cares if I stay in Brooklyn?" he asked one reporter. "Who cares if I wear sneakers, and ride subways, and don't have a driver's license? What difference does it make?"

DEVELOPING A STYLE

Lee's body of work is as complex as his personality. Some of his works cover unusual topics, far removed from one another, but all are based on real life and real people. *Crooklyn*, a snapshot of life and times in Lee's Brooklyn neighborhood, is called by some critics "his most affectionate work." *Clockers* is a crime drama where a career opportunity for one drug dealer results in a rival's murder. In *4 Little Girls*, Lee captures the lives and deaths, and speculates on the unreached potential, of four children killed in a racially motivated Alabama church bombing during the 1960s. He's also planning a biography about Jackie Robinson, the first black professional baseball player. In addition to films, Lee has written books and

Such films as Crooklyn, *left, focus on such issues as gang violence. A victim of a church bombing is displayed in* 4 Little Girls, *middle. Spike has acted in commercials, bottom, and has recently started a family with wife Tonya Lewis, opposite.*

directed TV commercials, specials, and music videos for some of the world's most recognized talent.

Lee married attorney Tonya Linette Lewis in October 1993. He has been reluctant to discuss their marriage and children, however. While he's always happy to share news of his public life, he keeps his private life private.

Fame has helped Lee get close to his sports heroes. Nike, the athletic shoe manufacturer, asked him to recreate his role of Mars Blackmon for a series of popular Air Jordan sneaker ads with basketball star Michael Jordan. He gets great seats at major sporting events, which he attends regularly, and he follows the New York Knicks basketball team with special zeal. "Truth is, Spike is no different from you or me in his rage for sports," noted a reporter, "except that when he yells at a Chicago Bulls game, 'Yo, way to house him, Michael!' Jordan looks at him and says, 'Thanks,' and then they have dinner together after the game."

Lee's stardom has not caused him to rest or take his work less seriously. He has not shied away from controversy, tackling such topics as interracial romance in *Jungle Fever* and the life of the well-known civil rights leader in *Malcolm X*. "Here's a man who rose up from the dregs of society," Lee said about Malcolm X, "spent time in jail, reeducated himself and, through spiritual enlightenment, rose to the top. This is an incredible story and I know it will inspire people."

Throughout his career he has used his media-star status to express his often unpopular views. For example, he has criticized white directors for failing to accurately depict the lives of blacks in their films. In fact, when he learned that a white director was originally planning to direct Malcolm X's story, he strongly voiced his disapproval and eventually gained control of the project. He has also lambasted other black entertainers for—

Never one to back away from heated issues, Spike Lee's work has included the controversial film Malcolm X.

in his view—not being true to their ethnic roots and not using their influence to line up jobs for fellow African-Americans. In 1988, he established the Spike Lee Minority Fellowship at the New York University film school.

Most of all, Lee has asked his audiences to wake up. He once said that the purpose of his often open-ended movies is to provoke awareness and thought about the problems we face in our society. His films insist that racism remains a prevalent force and demand that we acknowledge its brutality. And his films urge blacks—whom he sees as his primary audience—to fight to make their voices heard, and to take control of their own lives and fortunes, as he himself so skillfully has done.

Spike's passionate and sometimes unpopular approach to voicing black issues through the film industry is shared by fellow director John Singleton, left. A regular at New York Knicks' games, Spike's other passion is professional basketball.

V O I C E S

ON HIS CHILDHOOD:

"My mother was always taking me
places to see performing arts. I was
grounded in the arts. . . . [I] remem-
ber her taking me to Broadway to
see *The King and I* with Yul Brynner
when I was four or five years old,
and how I cried until she took me
home because I was too scared.
Either the music was too loud or I
didn't like our seats—last row in the
balcony. I'm still afraid of heights."

Spike Lee

"It was never easy for Spike to love his mother full-out. Jacquelyn was the
bad cop. Bill was the good cop. She was the disciplinarian, and he was
the lenient one. 'All of us liked our father better because there was never
any static coming from him,' Spike says. 'It would be like, "Daddy, can we
jump off the building?" "Yeah, go ahead.""

 Rick Reilly, reporter

"I understood from being my father's son that talent alone is not nearly
enough. My father has always been a greatly talented musician, but it
takes more than that. You've got to have business sense, too. . . . You can't
function well as a starving artist—at least, I knew I never wanted to try
and do that, and this was long before I became a successful filmmaker.
My father would come home with a suit, let's say. He'd say, 'Look here,
I got this suit for four hundred dollars,' swearing he got a bargain. My
brothers and I would look at each other and say, 'Man, that suit cost fifty
dollars. You got robbed! Aw man, Daddy. Not again. . . .'"

 Spike Lee

"One Saturday when we were [at the Lido Theater] checking out the matinee, some construction was going on right next door, and somebody drove a bulldozer through the wall during the movie! . . . And maybe that's one reason I ended up being the kind of filmmaker I became. I figure the competition might be a bulldozer coming through the wall, and I've got to keep my audience involved, or one day I won't be around, either."

Spike Lee

ON HIS PERSONALITY:

"I'm very happy. I'm happily married. I have a daughter. The Knicks fired their head coach. I'm very happy."

Spike Lee, 1996

"Diffusing anger with humor is Spike Lee's specialty, and it's a feat he performs best where his own public image is concerned. . . . The angry young man of press reports is always tempered by the characters Lee plays on-screen."

Peggy Orenstein, reporter

"Racism usually erodes self-confidence—it seems to have triggered his."

Ruby Dee, actor

Spike keeps his public life—which includes directorial and acting roles, media appearances, and film awards—very separate from his private family life with wife Tonya and daughter Satchel, below.

"So many people are offended by Spike because people—especially black people—want Spike to be Jesse Jackson, gregarious, give them that eye contact, the firm handshake. He's just not like that. He internalizes everything."

Nelson George, music editor and writer

An intense and resilient personality has allowed Spike Lee to succeed in working with issues that often have resulted in public criticism.

O N R A D I C A L I S S U E S :

"I've never really thought of myself as a spokesperson for thirty-five million African-Americans. . . . All my views have been solely my views, and I think that there are African-American people who agree with me, but we also have African-Americans who don't agree. . . . It is a fallacy that all of my critics are white."

Spike Lee

"I think [we black people have] done more to hold ourselves back than anybody. I've never been one to say, 'White man this, white man that. . . .' If anybody's seen all my films, I put most of the blame on our shoulders and say, 'Look, we're gonna have to do for ourselves.'"

Spike Lee

"Racism has been our biggest cancer, and until we deal with and acknowledge it, we're never going to be able to move forward and upward. They think, 'We've done enough for the niggers. They got Michael Jackson, they got Cosby, they got Arsenio Hall;' and their perception is that because a couple of people were able to slip through the cracks, it's like that for thirty-five million Americans, but the truth is that the African underclass now is larger than it's ever been."

Spike Lee

⬤N FILMMAKING:

"Fever. We all had it bad. We were on a mission. We wanted to make films that captured the black experience in this country—films about what we knew. We just couldn't wait."

Ernest Dickerson,
cinematographer

A belief in moving toward positive change in the African-American community has been the driving force behind the film career of Spike Lee.

"The most that Spike ever tells an actor is, 'Here's the script. Ready? Action!' And it used to be very funny for me to watch the seasoned veterans say, 'Well, Spike, what is your vision?' Spike says, 'I paid you good money to act. That's my vision. Now act. Action!'"

    Branford Marsalis, musician

"Most of the movies that people are used to . . . [are] the same old formula, and at the end of the movie everything is wrapped up in a nice little bow. Very rarely do those movies ever make you think, and once you leave the theater, by the time you're back on the subway or driving home, you've forgotten what you watched. It's like disposable entertainment. You sit there for two hours, and it washes over you and that's it."

    Spike Lee

"Lee's films differ not only in their black perspective—in an industry where few blacks have a voice—but also in their ability to look at both sides of the coin at once. As in real life, his characters are neither all good nor all bad. And therein lies their—and Lee's—power: the minute he establishes our identification with a character, Lee turns him inside out to reveal the dark side in us."

Marlaine Glicksman, reporter

"I'm not going to get up here and say, 'Do this, do that, that's the right thing.' I just want people to think."

Spike Lee

"A lot of African-Americans are so hungry for the next savior, next leader, that they transfer these leadership qualities to athletes and entertainers. Oprah [Winfrey] is a great role model, but if you ask her, 'Are you [the next] Martin Luther King or Malcolm X?' she'll tell you she's not."

Spike Lee

Like the outspoken Malcolm X, portrayed by Denzel Washington, left, in Lee's film biography of the slain civil rights leader, Spike strives to be a vocal leader for the black community today.

OVATIONS